NEW DYSLEXIA-FRIENDLY
EARLY CHAPTER BOOKS!
READING LEVEL GRADES 1-2

NOW AVAILABLE IN CANADA AND THE US!

What makes these books dyslexia friendly?

Font

This series uses a dyslexia-friendly font called OpenDyslexic. OpenDyslexic is a new open source font created to help with some of the symptoms of dyslexia. Letters have heavy-weighted bottoms to indicate direction and help readers quickly figure out which part of the letter is down, which helps readers from rotating them around. The unique shapes of the letters can help prevent confusion caused by flipping and swapping letters.

This font is being updated continually and improved based on input from dyslexic users. To learn more about OpenDyslexic, **visit the website**.

Paper stock

These books use cream-coloured paper which is recommended for dyslexic readers instead of white paper. The paper stock is also matte, instead of glossy, and is a heavier stock to prevent any glaring through from the other side of the page.

Layout

The layout of pages in a book is important to dyslexia readers. Both the lines and paragraphs are kept short to avoid dense blocks of text. There is lots of spacing between lines and paragraphs and wide margins and headers are used to break up the text. Hyphenation isn't used for words that aren't usually split, and lines are kept left justified with a ragged edge.

more titles in

The Secret Games of Maximus Todd!

Hyper to the Max

Clever Max invents a game to keep his Super Fidgets at bay for the day. Too bad his arch enemy Mandy Beth discovers what he's up to and tries to trip him up! Will Max win at his secret game?

Frantic Friend Countdown

Max has a dilemma. Everyone's got a best friend except him. But when a new kid arrives at the school, Max plays a secret game to make him Max's buddy. Too bad the new kid would rather hang out with barf-breath Mandy Beth, peskiest pest in the entire town!

Big Game Jitters

It's the soccer championship and Max's team is playing the school bully's team. Of course, as soon as the match starts, Max's gets a case of the Super Fidgets. If Max can't invent a secret game to calm them, it might cost his team the championship

Flu Shot

by L. M. Nicodemo

illustrated by Graham Ross

Fidgets

Formac Publishing Company Limited
Halifax

Formac Publishing Company Limited recognizes the support of the Province
of Nova Scotia through Film and Creative Industries Nova Scotia. We are
pleased to work in partnership with the Province of Nova Scotia to develop
and promote our creative industries for the benefit of all Nova Scotians. We
acknowledge the support of the Canada Council for the Arts which last year
invested $157 million to bring the arts to Canadians throughout the country.

Cover design: Meghan Collins
Cover image: Graham Ross

Library and Archives Canada Cataloguing in Publication

Nicodemo, L. M., author
        Flu shot fidgets / L.M. Nicodemo ; illustrated by Graham Ross.

(The secret games of Maximus Todd)
ISBN 978-1-4595-0434-9 (hardback)

        I. Ross, Graham, 1962-, illustrator II. Title.

PS8627.I245F58 2016   jC813'.6   C2015-907254-9

Formac Publishing Company Limited   Distributed in the United States by:
5502 Atlantic Street   Lerner Publishing Group
Halifax, Nova Scotia, Canada   1251 Washington Ave N
B3H 1G4   Minneapolis, MN, USA
www.formac.ca   55401

Printed and bound in Canada.

Manufactured by Friesens Corporation in Altona, Manitoba, Canada in
May 2016.

Job #222737

Contents

Chapter One

Nervous

Tick . . . tock . . . tick . . . tock. Maximus Todd kicked his feet in time to the office clock and then shifted in his chair. Again.

Principal Hagglefinster looked up from the papers on her desk.

"Your mother will be here soon, Mr. Todd," she said, peering over her half-moon glasses.

Max shifted once more, making his chair scrape the floor. *Squeech.*

"How about you water the plants for me?" she asked. "Here's the can. You can fill it at the fountain."

Max got up. "SURE," he said loudly. Making his voice go big like that felt really good.

"Mmm, Ta-Ta-Ta, Mmm, Ta-Ta-Ta,"

Max hummed his worry hum as he headed down the school's

empty hallway. At the fountain, he shoved the plastic can under the spout and pressed the lever.

WHERE IS MOM? he wondered. He had a doctor's appointment today. She was supposed to pick him up at school right after basketball practice.

WHY ISN'T SHE HERE YET?

Maybe she forgot.

Boy, would that be fine, thought Max hopefully. *Double fudge fine.*

For Max, going to the doctor's was like having ten hours of homework PLUS ten

hours of piano practice! He
hated the waiting room — it
smelled weird. And there was
always some baby crying.

He hated getting poked and prodded.

"OPEN YOUR MOUTH."

"OPEN YOUR NOSE."

"OPEN YOUR EARS."

What was the doctor looking for, anyway?

Most of all, Max hated
the shots. They were scary.
Monster-under-the-bed
terrifying. Would he be getting
one today? His stomach did a
nervous flip.

Suddenly Max's shirt
sleeve felt wet. The can was
overflowing, spilling water
everywhere.

"Ah, geesh," he moaned.

When Max got back to the office, his mother was waiting for him. Ms. Hagglefinster told Max to leave the watering to her.

"YOU DON'T WANT TO BE LATE,"

she said in a voice that sounded like she was glad to see him finally go.

Chapter Two

Stuck with mandy Beth

"SORRY I'M LATE," Max's mother said as they rushed to the car. The sky was dark with storm clouds. Any minute the rain would come. "I had to pick up Mandy Beth from her dance class. Her parents will be getting in a little late from work."

"Aw, Mom," Max groaned. "Not Mandy Beth! You said Shiv could come over." Shiv Pal was Max's new friend from school.

Mom pulled Max along. "Yes, Max, if you behave at the doctor's, Shiv will come over. I'll take Mandy Beth home after your appointment. Her parents will be back by then." Mom paused.

"THOUGH i DON'T KNOW WHY SHE CAN'T JOIN iN WITH YOU BOYS."

Max frowned. How could
he tell Mom that Mandy Beth
Bokely was the biggest pest
in the school? Possibly in the
whole town? Maybe even in the
entire country?

She'd never believe him.
Mandy Beth fooled every
grown-up he knew.

When he reached the car,

Mom unlocked the door and Max slid into the back seat. Just then, thunder cracked and the sky burst open with rain.

"Hey, Max," Mandy Beth said. She was already strapped in. A book lay open on her lap.

"Don't bug me, *Mangy Breath*," Max replied. "I have to sit and think about my appointment. It's a checkup, so it's VERY serious."

Mandy Beth stuck out her tongue. Then she turned back to the book she'd been reading.

Swish, swish, swish. Back and forth went the wipers. Mom gripped the steering wheel and drove. Outside, the rain pelted down.

All of a sudden, Max's arm started to itch. From underneath his jacket sleeve, he could feel his wet shirt. It was all bunched up. Max squirmed and pulled at the fabric.

"Can you please stop moving

around," Mandy Beth said, loud
enough for Max's mom to hear.
"I'm trying to read and you're
making my page jiggle."

Max glared. He didn't have
to listen to her.

"MOM, ARE WE
THERE YET?"

he asked, yanking this way and
that at the wedged-up cloth.

"Almost, Max," Mom
answered, her eyes glued on
the road. "This weather is
making everyone drive slowly.
No one wants an accident."

Max frowned and stared
out the window. He tried not
to think about his wet sleeve.

Then he tried not to think
about the doctor. And the
waiting room. And the maybe
shot.

Suddenly, Max's legs began
to quake and his feet to shake.
The sound of the rain faded as
a new noise came into his head.
It was like a jet plane landing
in his brain.

This could only mean one thing — an attack of the SUPER FIDGETS!

Every now and then Max got so

FIDGETY AND JITTERY AND TWITCHY

that he could NOT sit still. Not for a chocolate brownie with coloured sprinkles. Not for a special edition *Cyborgs of Justice* comic book.

The only way Max could manage was to make up a secret game to play in his head. If he was busy on the inside, he'd be less hyper on the outside.

"Max!" called Mom when they were stopped at a red traffic light. "You're as jumpy as a frog back there. The whole car is shaking. Try to relax."

"Yeah," chimed in Mandy

Beth. "It's like an earthquake."

Max made EXTRA sharp dagger eyes at her. But she was the least of his problems.

He had done some quick calculations in his head:

CAN'T SIT STILL = TROUBLE AT THE DOCTOR'S

TROUBLE AT THE DOCTOR'S = MOM GETS MAD

MOM GETS MAD = NO SHIV

Boy, I need a game, he thought. He squeezed his eyes shut and concentrated.

Jumpy as a frog . . . Jumpy as a frog . . . That was it!

"Ribbit. Ribbit." Max croaked. Mom chuckled. Mandy Beth shook her head and went back to her book.

Chapter Three

Critters stop the Jitters

Finally they arrived at the large, grey medical building. Mom huddled Max and Mandy Beth under the umbrella.

"Am I going to get a shot, Mom?" Max asked as they crossed the wet parking lot.

"We'll have to wait and see, Max," his mother said.

Max shuddered. That means **PROBABLY**.

The entrance was a double door made of glass. Max could see people gathered around it, looking out. Nobody wanted to leave. They were all waiting for the rain to stop.

A man from inside opened the door as they came near. "Oh thank you," his mother said.

"You're welcome," he answered. "It sure is raining cats and dogs out there, isn't it?"

Mom laughed. "It sure is!"

Max's ears pricked up. *Cats and dogs?* Already, the game was underway. "Meow, woof," he muttered into his jacket collar.

"What's that, my guy?" Mom asked.

"Nothing, Mom. Just a cough." Max cleared his throat to make it seem true.

"KWOOF, KWOOF."

Mom put her hand on Max's forehead. "Hey. You aren't getting sick, are you?"

Max shook his head. "No, no. Just swallowed the wrong way."

"That was no cough!" Mandy Beth hissed at him. She looked confused. Max squinched up his face. It was none of her business!

Down the hall they went, with his mother leading the way. Outside Dr. Krumper's office door, she paused.

"Remember, young man, there are sick people in there. They do not need to be

bothered with any silliness."
Mom was serious. "Once we're
in, I want you to be as quiet as
a mouse. Got it?"

Mouse? Max nodded. "Uh huh
. . . squeak, squeak."

Though he had kept his
voice low, Mandy Beth heard
him and giggled. Max's mother
heard him too. She did not look
amused.

"i need you to behave, Max. Otherwise, Shiv will not be coming over."

"I'll be good, Mom. I promise," Max insisted.

I WILL be good, he thought, *now that I have my game.*

It seemed like a sure win. All Max had to do was pay attention to people talking. If someone mentioned an animal, he would make its sound.

This might actually be fun.

Except if he lost. Because if he did, he would tell Mom that he wanted Mandy Beth to stay over rather than Shiv.

Ugh. Max winced. *I better not lose.*

Chapter Four

Horses and Pigs

When they entered the doctor's office, Max's mother went over to the front desk to sign in. She signalled Max and Mandy Beth to find a place to sit.

Though it was crowded, Max

spotted a couple of empty
seats. On one side was a
mother holding a crying baby.
Max rolled his eyes. *Figures.*
On the other side was an
elderly lady knitting a mitten.
He sat down, saved a seat for
his mother and pointed to a

distant chair for Mandy Beth.

"Thanks a lot," Mandy Beth
muttered. She plopped down
on a chair in the corner and
opened her book.

In no time, Max began to
feel restless. The wet sleeve
was itchy again. He drummed
his fingers and tapped his feet.
Mom gave him a settle-down
look.

For all the so-called sickness, it was not a quiet waiting room. People were talking. Max could catch scraps of their conversations.

But no one was saying anything about animals. *Too bad Dr. Krumper's not a vet,* mused Max.

"Ed, I'm worried about your

leg," a woman across from Max said to the man next to her.

"Oh, it's nothing, my dear," he answered, patting her hand. "Probably just a charley horse."

Horse! Ah ha! Max thought for a minute. Then he turned to his mother. "Good thing Shiv lives in our NEIGHbourhood. WHINNY comes over, we're going to have lots of fun."

Max's mom smiled. Mandy Beth overheard and rolled her eyes.

The woman continued. "You know, you might have to quit golfing for a bit. If the doctor says it's best."

"Quit golfing?" The man did not like the idea at all. "When pigs fly!"

Pigs?!? Another animal! Max tried to think of a sentence that he could say with the word "oink." Nothing came to mind. He decided to hide it in a sneeze. A fake sneeze.

"AHH-CHOINK,"

he sneezed, covering his mouth with his sleeve.

Mom looked at him. She was wearing her worried eyebrows. "First a cough. Now a sneeze. You might be coming down with something, Max."

"No big deal, Mom. My nose felt ticklish. That's all." He gave her a smile to show he was absolutely fine.

Chapter Five

Quackers

"WaH, WaH," the baby next to Max bawled. The baby's mother was rocking him back and forth. Max often saw his own mother do the same with his baby sister, Sarah, if she was fussy. Sometimes it worked.

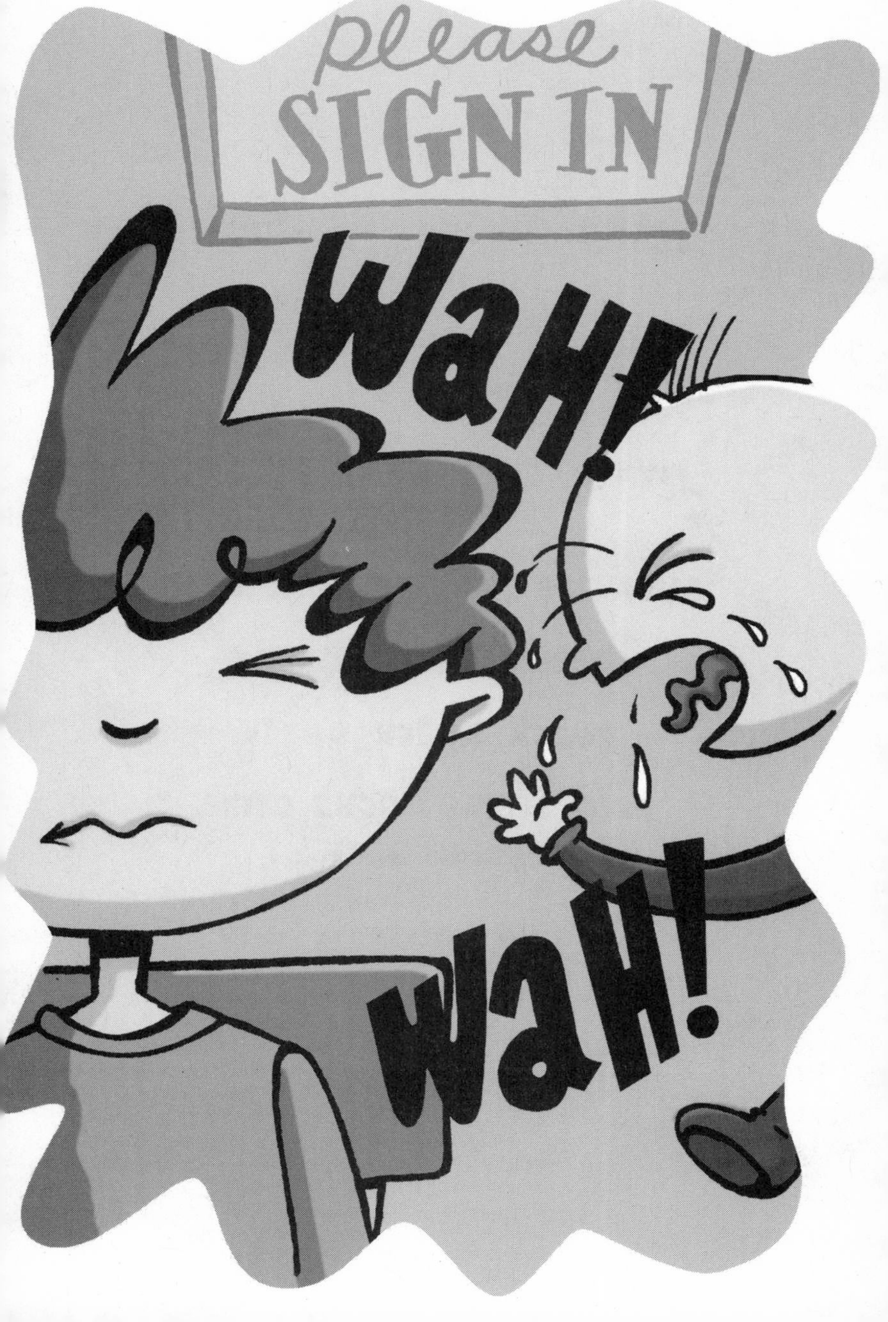
please
SIGN IN
WAH!
WAH!

Sometimes it didn't.

With this baby, it wasn't working.

The mom began singing softly:

FIVE LITTLE DUCKS WENT OUT ONE DAY,

OVER THE HILLS AND FAR AWAY.

MAMA DUCK CALLED

— QUACK, QUACK, QUACK —

FOUR LITTLE DUCKS CAME SWIMMING BACK . . .

Max could not believe his ears. *Ducks!*

"Quack, quack, quack," he said in a low voice.

The mom looked over and
smiled, thinking that Max was
trying to help. She continued,
nodding at him to join in. "Four
little ducks went out one
day . . ."

When the "quack, quack, quack" part came, Max quietly quacked too, doing his best to sound like a duck. The baby looked over and kept his eyes on Max.

"Quack, quack, quack," said Max again. The baby stopped his crying altogether.

Finally the song finished. Max had quacked at every part. And now the baby was fast asleep.

"Thanks for helping to settle my baby," said the mother.

The old woman who was knitting joined in. "Nice work, young man. I thought you

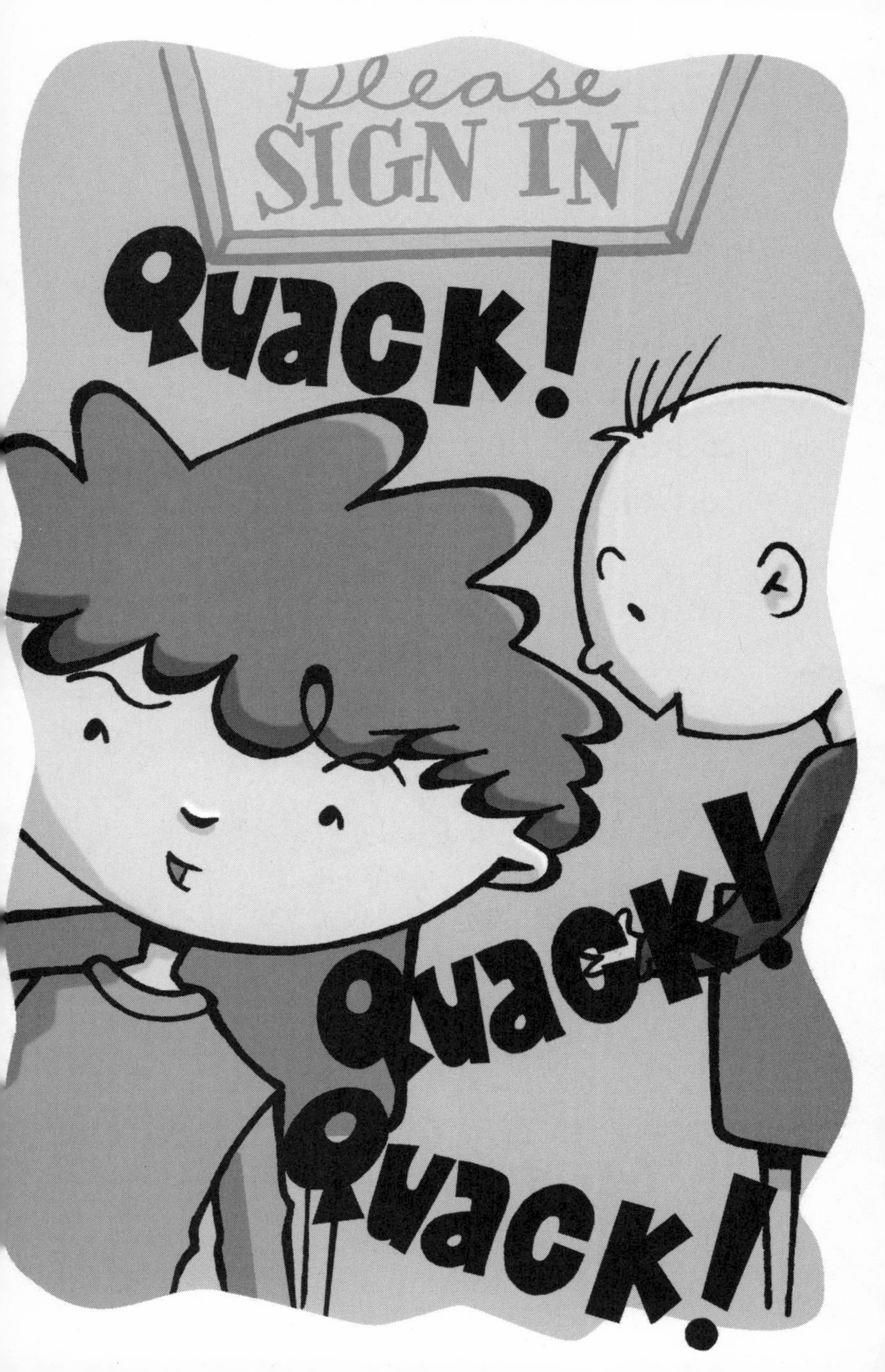
Please
SIGN IN
QUACK!
QUACK!
QUACK!

sounded like a real duck."

"Quack," he said, hopefully for the last time. The old woman chuckled and returned to her knitting. Max smiled. He felt like a hero.

Chapter Six

Sounds Like a Barn in Here

Max stretched out his legs and
wondered when his name would
be called. Now that the baby
was asleep, the waiting room
had turned quiet. TOO quiet.
Max could sense his *Super
Fidgets* building up again.

He felt like a cork ready to
POP.

Just then, the waiting room
door opened. Max looked up.
Who should walk in but Dana
Daminski, his reading partner
from school! She was with her
father. She smiled shyly at Max
and waved at Mandy Beth.

Max smiled back. Dana was nice, even though she was a girl. For some reason, Max always had butterflies in his stomach when she was around. He kind of liked the feeling.

Is she sick? Maybe she's getting a shot. Right away he was sorry for her.

Once Dana was seated, Max got up the courage to speak to her.

"Hi Dana. I'm here for a checkup. Pretty serious. Might have to get a shot."

Dana nodded.

"I'm not scared though," Max continued. "Oh no! I've had hundreds of shots. No big deal."

He realized that was a bit of a lie. But it didn't seem right to let Dana know how frightened he really was. "HUNDREDS!" he repeated more loudly.

Unfortunately, Max's voice woke up the baby. It began to fuss again. **"WAAAH."**

Mandy Beth suddenly spoke up. She had been so quiet that Max had forgotten she was there. "I know a song that your baby might like," she said to the mother. "What about 'Old MacDonald'? Your baby seems to like animal sounds and my friend Max is good at making them."

"That's a great suggestion," the mother replied.

"DO YOU KNOW 'OLD MacDONALD'?"

She turned to Max.

Max was too stunned to say anything. *Darn that pesky Mandy Beth!*

"What's wrong, Max?" Mandy Beth teased. "Cat got your tongue?"

Cat?!? Max's teeth clenched. *Oooh. I'm gonna make her pay for this!*

"No," said Max. "I'm PURR-fectly fine."

"Of course he knows the

song," Max's mom spoke for him. "And he'd be happy to sing it. Isn't that right, my guy?"

Red splotches exploded on Max's cheeks. From the corner of his eye, he saw Dana watching. What could he do?

The mother began singing "Old MacDonald." And because of Max's game, he had to make every animal sound listed in the song.

He tweeted and howled, bleated and brayed, hooted and honked, squealed and squawked.

He was not brave enough to look over at Dana, but he hoped she wasn't listening. He had never been so embarrassed in his whole life.

They were on goats when the nurse behind the desk announced, "Maximus Todd."

Finally. Max had never thought he'd be so happy to see Dr. Krumper. He got up quickly and, without glancing at Dana, followed his mother to the examination room. Luckily, Mandy Beth had to stay behind.

I hope she catches something that makes her itch all over, Max silently wished.

Chapter Seven

Weighed and measured

Nurse Chou greeted Max and his mother, "Nice to see you again." She led them to a small room. It had a sink, a desk, a couple of chairs and a long examination table.

"I think we've been

growing," she said, glancing up from her clipboard.

Max had long ago noticed that Nurse Chou muddled some of her words. She said "we" a lot. But sometimes it meant "I" and sometimes it meant "you." Strangely, it never meant "us."

"Yes I think we've been growing," she repeated.

She means ME, thought Max.
Nurse Chou was too old to
grow anymore.

"Just like . . ." she continued.

Max's eyes grew wide and he
held his breath.

iS SHE GOiNG TO name an animaL? WHAT animaL GROWS FAST? A SnaKe? A WHaLe? A GORiLLa?

His heart skipped a beat.

"A weed," she finished. Max
let out a sigh.

"Now, we'll get weighed and
measured," said Nurse Chou.

Max nodded. *I'LL get
weighed and measured.*

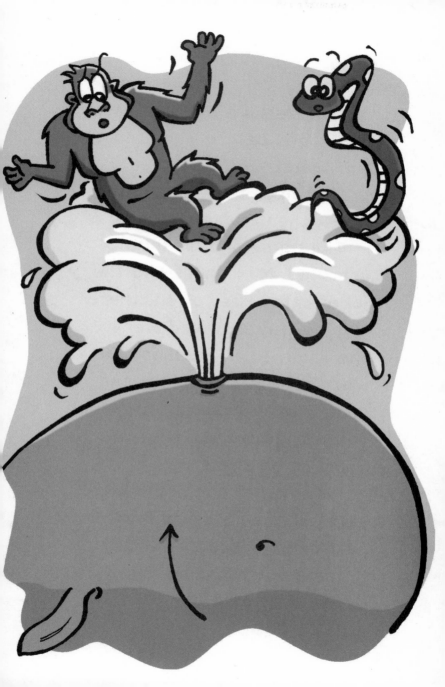

"Please take off your jacket and shoes before you step on the scale, Max. We don't want Dr. Krumper thinking she's got an elephant for a patient."

The nurse and his mother chuckled. Max didn't find the joke funny. First of all, there was no way he could weigh the same as an elephant. He was too thin and lanky. And second, Max now had to make an elephant sound. How was he going to do that?

He covered his mouth and fake-coughed a short bray, "Brrraahh — cough — cough." It came out sounding like a

broken trumpet. Max felt silly.

"Are you coming down with something, Max?" asked the nurse.

"Can you check?" asked Max's mother. "That's the second time he's made a strange cough since we got here. And he's been sneezing, too."

"Make sure to let the Doctor know," Nurse Chou Said.

After the weigh-in, Max stood against a post marked like a giant ruler. The nurse gently lowered a metal arm onto his head. It had an arrow that pointed to a measurement on the post.

"My, my," Nurse Chou said as she recorded Max's height. "You're getting to be as tall as a giraffe."

Max looked up at her. He thought carefully for a minute and then said nothing. He wasn't sure if giraffes made any sounds. But all the giraffes he'd seen on TV were quiet. *Phew!*

"Am I going to get a shot?" he asked Nurse Chou.

"We'll have to wait and see," she answered.

That means I have to wait and see. SHE already knows. Max groaned. *I PROBABLY have to get a shot.*

"Hop onto the table, Max. Dr. Krumper will be here shortly." Nurse Chou left the room.

"I'm going to check on Mandy Beth," Max's mom said. "I'll be right back."

The door closed and Max leaped off the table. He needed

to MOVE. Though he was
playing his game,

He STiLL FeLT aLL SQUiRMY inSiDe.

It's because of the
shot, Max realized.

He jogged around the
little room three times. Next
he gazed at the posters on
the wall. One had a picture
of a real heart, cut in half.
Another showed the inside of a
stomach.

Guts are sooo cool, thought Max.

Then he took a look at the pamphlets. Dr. Krumper sure had a lot. He opened one up. Too many words. **BORiNG.**

Just then, he heard the door creak. With a hop, skip and a jump, Max was back on the table.

Chapter Eight

The Shot

The door opened wide and in walked Mom. Dr. Krumper followed. She wore a white lab coat. Her doctor's pants had pictures of moons and stars on them. Around her neck was a stethoscope.

"Well, Max," said Dr. Krumper, "let's see how you're doing today."

Max tried to not feel nervous. Instead, he thought about his game. *Would the doctor say the name of an animal?*

Most likely.

Dr. Krumper placed a flat stick against his tongue and peered down his throat.

"Aaahhh," said the doctor. "Aaahhh," repeated Max.

Then she shone a light into Max's eyes. She used another light to look

in his nose, ears and mouth.
"Any bats in there?" the doctor
joked.

An animal! "Screek, screek,"
Max joked back.

Mom showed Max her please-
behave face. But the doctor
laughed.

She thumped on his
chest and listened with her
stethoscope. After that, she
made Max raise his arms and
cough.

"Almost done," Dr. Krumper
said as she entered information
on her computer.

Max was shocked. The
checkup had been easy! In fact,
too easy . . .

The doctor turned back to
Max.

**"OKAY, MAX, i need
TO GIVE YOU a FLU
SHOT now."**

I KNEW IT! thought Max. His heart began to beat wildly.

"Don't worry. I've got this new kind of needle. **YOU'LL HARDLY FEEL IT,**" she promised.

Max wanted to be tough. He rolled up his sleeve and looked away. His insides were churning like a bubbling soup.

"It really doesn't hurt at all," Dr. Krumper assured him. "Not even a bee sting."

Bee?!? Is a bee an animal? Or, is it only an insect? But, is an insect an animal? Should he buzz? Max wasn't sure.

"All done," the doctor

suddenly announced. "Good job!"

Huh!?! Max hadn't felt a thing. Thinking about bees and insects and animals had distracted him from feeling the shot.

"Gee, it kind of hurtzzzz," he said to the doctor, sneaking in some buzzing. Just in case.

"Really?" she asked. "I think you just want a treat."

The doctor reached under the desk and pulled out a box. She turned to Max. "Here, Max. Pick something from the treasure chest. You've been a good patient today."

Max grinned. This was the

ONE awesome thing about visiting Dr. Krumper. She had a super-cool treat bin.

He rummaged through the pile of goodies and found a *Cyborgs of Justice* decoder ring.

"THANKS A LOT, DR. KRUMPER," he said, putting on the ring. It fit perfectly. He felt wildly happy. *I'm all done! Looks like Shiv will be coming over!*

Chapter Nine

A Riddle

Dr. Krumper turned to Max's mother. "Are there any concerns? If not, we're finished here."

Max jumped down from the examination table. He was more than ready to go.

"Oh, yes!" said Mom. "Max

has been having these strange coughs and sneezes since we got here. Is he coming down with something?"

Max's cheeks reddened. The coughs and sneezes had been phony. He felt bad that he was making his mother worry.

Mom continued. "Max is supposed to have a friend visit. But I don't want him to make anyone else ill."

The doctor shook her head. "I think Max is fine, Ms. Todd. However, it might be allergies. You know, to dust or pollen. Let's make another appointment to look into it."

Another appointment! Max
moaned. *Oh well! At least my
checkup is done.*

Now Dr. Krumper had one
hand on the doorknob. She was
finally leaving. Max held still.
*Goodbye, Dr. Krumper. See you
later, alligator. Ta-ta for now.*

But suddenly she stopped.
"Oh gee, I almost forgot!" She
tapped her forehead. "I've got

a riddle for you Max, and it's a good one!"

Max smiled weakly. Dr. Krumper always had a joke. Between the treat bin and the joke, it was hard not to like her. *Please let it NOT be about animals.*

Dr. Krumper's eyes twinkled. Max could tell she was trying hard to hold back a laugh.

"can you tell me, max, how does a cow get to mars?"

A *cow!?!* Max stiffened. *Really? The joke is about an animal? Now he'd have to moo somehow.*

I'm in a great MOO-D. Let's
go to the MOO-VIES. Hip hop
MOO-SIC is my favourite.

Nothing worked.

Dr. Krumper's face leaned
closer to Max. "Do you give
up?" she asked.

He could always sneeze
again. *Ah-chMOO!* But his
mother would cancel Shiv's
visit. For sure.

If he didn't moo, he'd lose his game! Either way, Shiv wasn't going to come over. Max realized he was trapped.

Chapter Ten

Things Don't Always Work Out

Max glanced at his mother
and then back at the doctor.
What could he do with a moo?
He was almost ready to call
it quits when he noticed Dr.
Krumper's pants. All at once,
Max knew what to say.

"By jumping over the MOO-N!" he shouted a bit too loudly.

"Hey, that's pretty good," laughed Dr. Krumper. "But it's not the answer."

She broke out into a fit of giggles. "It's by flying through UDDER space!" she said. "Oh, that one always cracks me up!"

Max laughed, too. Mostly out of relief, but the doctor didn't need to know that.

Back in the waiting room, Mandy Beth asked, "How did your checkup go?

DiD YOU GeT a SHOT?"

Max refused to talk to her. She had embarrassed him in front of the one girl in his whole class that he didn't think had cooties. *Mandy Beth can go sit in a field of poison ivy.*

"It went fine, Mandy Beth," his mom answered. "It's nice of you to ask."

As they were leaving, Max snuck a look over at Dana. She gave him a little wave. She didn't seem bothered that he'd sung "Old MacDonald" to the baby. He was glad.

Outside, the sun peeked out from behind the grey clouds.

The rain had stopped. Max felt excited. He'd won his game.

And now, Shiv was coming over!

All they had to do was drop Mandy Beth off at her house. Max leaned back in his seat. It was nice no longer having to bark or bleat or bray.

"You know, Max, you're very lucky to have a friend like Mandy Beth," his mother said as she turned the car into their neighbourhood.

"MMPH," SNORTED MAX. HE WOULD NOT, COULD NOT, AGREE.

Mom went on. "Well, I think that Mandy Beth should stay over for the evening. She deserves a bit of fun after waiting all that time at Dr. Krumper's."

Max's jaw dropped. What was his mother thinking?

"How about it, Mandy Beth?" Mom asked.

Max shook his head furiously

at Mandy Beth, whose lips were curled into a sneaky smile. He silently mouthed NO and sent her super mean looks with his eyes.

It didn't matter.

"That sounds great, Ms. Todd," replied Mandy Beth. "And I promise I'll keep the boys in line for you." She smirked at Max. "No **MONKEY** business!"

Mom laughed. "Wonderful. And what do you have to say to that, Max?"

For a few seconds, Max was speechless. With Mandy Beth weaselling in, his

SPECTACULAR WIN WAS NOW a GIGANTIC FAIL!

And there was nothing he could do about it.

So he scratched under his armpits and stamped his feet. Then he reached over to Mandy Beth's hair and pretended to pull out a bug and eat it.

"Oooh. Oooh. Aaah. Aaah," Max answered his mother in his best chimp voice.

What else could he say?